the Witch Switch

by Anne Harler

illustrated by Bob Doty

Willowisp Press

Published by Willowisp Press, Inc.
401 E. Wilson Bridge Road, Worthington, Ohio 43085

Copyright © 1987 by Willowisp Press, Inc.

Printed in the United States of America
10 9 8 7 6 5 4 3 2 1

ISBN 0-87406-245-4

Once there was a girl named Wendy. She lived with her parents.

Wendy's hair was always tangled.
She could hardly comb it.
When she was in a hurry,
she would say a few abracadabras.
Then her tangles would straighten.

Magic was easy for Wendy.
Wendy was a witch.
Being eight was fun.
But being eight and
being a witch like her mom
was the most fun of all.

Her mom always planned
something magic for
them to do after school.
At least her mom used to.
Then something changed all that.

"Wendy, wait for me,"
her friend, Zelda,
called after school.
"What are you and your mom
going to do this afternoon?"
Zelda asked.

"Nothing," Wendy said,
kicking a rock.

"But, you two always do fun things."

"Not anymore," Wendy said.
"Not since the baby came."

"Never?" Zelda asked.

"Never." Wendy kicked another rock. "It's 'Miranda this' and 'Miranda that' all the time. All Mom does is take care of the baby. She wants me to think up my own fun now."

"Let me know if you
need any help," Zelda said.
She waved. Then she turned
up her street. Wendy walked
down to Witchway Lane.

I need Mom's help,
Wendy thought.
I cannot think up anything.
I do not have enough power for
new tricks, yet.
After all, my magic witch power
is only eight years old.
It's not nearly as old
as Mom's.

Wendy closed the kitchen
door behind her.

"Hi, Mom," she said.
"Can you go on a short
broomstick ride before
supper?"

"No, dear. You'll have
to go by yourself,"
her mom said. "I have
to feed Miranda in a
few minutes."

Just then Miranda began
to cry.

"Please rock the baby.
I'll warm her milk," her mom said.

Wendy went into Miranda's bedroom.
She rocked the cradle.

"Before you came along,
Mom and I had lots of fun,"
Wendy said. She stared down
at the baby. Her hair was
as tangly as Wendy's.

"We took long broomstick rides.
We stopped for batwing burgers.
We went to magic matinees on
Saturdays and learned to
do the neatest tricks.
Now look what's happened."

"Glub," said baby Miranda.
"Gurgle, glunk, glub."
Wendy sighed. At first
having a baby sister was fun.
Miranda hardly ever made a fuss,
except when she was hungry.

How can she take up
so much of Mom's time then?
Wendy wondered. It sure is
easy being a baby.
All you do is lie in bed
and say dumb stuff like
gurgle and glub.

Her mom hurried into the bedroom.
She had the baby's bottle of
magic milk.

"Be a good little witch, Wendy.
Run along now," her mom said.
"Think of something clever
and magic to do."

Wendy walked slowly outdoors.
She sat on her broom.
Then she tried to think of
something clever.

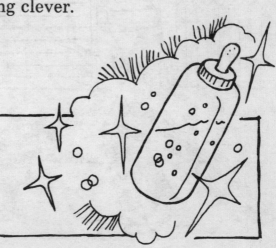

Would it be clever to move
the garage from one corner of
the yard to another? she wondered.
Wendy closed her eyes.

She said the words she had
learned at the last magic matinee.
   "Switchery, witchery, slithery, slot.
   Move the garage all over the lot."
Wendy opened her eyes.

She saw that nothing had happened.
The garage was still in the
same old place.
   Oh, well, she thought,
so much for clever.

Her dad came home from work.
Wendy rushed up to him.

"Will you play ball with me
before supper?" she asked.

"In a little while," he said.
"Let's go play with Miranda first,
before she goes to sleep."

Wendy sighed. She followed
her dad into Miranda's room.

That night Wendy went to bed
thinking. She wished she were
a baby again. It seemed to be
the nicest thing in the world to be.

Moms and dads hug and love and
feed their babies, she thought.
Babies do not have to pick up
their clothes. They do not
have to do homework. All they
do is gurgle and glub
and wait for their next meal.

Suddenly, Wendy sat
straight up in bed.

Wishes are magic, she thought.
Maybe I can't make the
garage switch places. But
maybe I can switch places
with Miranda.

Wendy closed her eyes and
said the magic words.

"*Magic power come my way.*
Make me someone else today."
Then it began to happen.

Slowly, oh so slowly,
Wendy felt herself growing smaller.
Then, she was all warm and
cuddly in Miranda's long
nighty-night with
bunny rabbits on it.
Wendy was a baby now.
Wendy was Miranda!

"Gurgle, glub," baby Wendy said.
That's all I can say, Wendy
thought. But, I can still
think with eight-year-old words.

Wendy hoped Miranda liked the
monster pajamas she had
been wearing. Then Wendy fell
asleep in the crib that
had been Miranda's.

In the morning, baby Wendy awoke.
She began to cry.
A minute later her mom
was leaning over the crib.
   "Good morning, dear," she said.
"Are you hungry?"

"Glunk," baby Wendy said.
Soon Wendy was drinking warm
magic milk from a bottle.

I'd rather have a doughnut,
she thought. Then Wendy remembered
that she didn't have any teeth.

Miranda, instead of Wendy,
left for school.

Good, baby Wendy thought.
Now I have Mom all to myself.
Soon her mom gave her a bath.
Then it was time for a nap.
But, she didn't mind.
Switching places last night had
made her very tired. When
she awoke, there was another
bottle of milk.

Baby Wendy took another
afternoon nap. Then she sat up
in the playpen. She looked out
the window. She saw Miranda
coming home from school.
Some of the kids from Wendy's
class were with her.
They were laughing and talking.
    I wonder what they are
saying, Wendy thought.
I wonder what they are
laughing about.

When her dad came home,
he held baby Wendy.
He gave her another bottle of milk.
Her mom and Miranda were making
chocolate chip cookies.

Yummm, baby Wendy thought.
Then she remembered she
could not chew chocolate chip
cookies, either.

Babies go to bed before
all the good TV programs,
Wendy thought. She lay awake
in the crib and listened.
She heard her dad and
Miranda laughing while her
mom popped popcorn.
Her mom said abracadabras
over it. The kernels leaped
all over the place.

I think I want to be
the older me, Wendy sighed.

She closed her eyes.
Then she began to repeat:
   "Magic power come my way.
   Make me someone else today."

I want to be the older me,
she thought again.
I want to be just plain
eight-year-old me. But
nothing happened, nothing at all.
Wendy was still the baby.
Miranda was out in the family
room being the older sister.

Wendy let out a cry
as she realized what had happened.

I don't have the magic
because I'm the baby now,
she thought. Maybe I will
have to grow up to be
eight years old all over again.
Baby Wendy cried louder.

Her mom rushed in and
picked her up.

"There, there, dear,"
she whispered. "Do not cry.
Mommy's here."

I wish I could have some
popcorn, baby Wendy thought.
Her mom gave her another bottle
of warm magic milk.

Grandma Witch arrived on
Friday to baby-sit. Wendy's mom
and dad were going to enjoy
a weekend holiday.

"Good-bye," Grandma called.
"I'll take good care of the
children."

Wendy's mom and dad flew off.

It is going to be super boring
now, baby Wendy thought.
Grandma will sing the same old
witch songs I have heard for
eight years. Here she comes.

"Hello, little baby,"
Grandma cooed.
She picked up baby Wendy.

46

They began to rock in the rocking chair. Baby Wendy began to sneeze.

"Oh, dear me," Grandma said. "My magic witch powder is making you sneeze. I don't have as much power as I used to. That's why I use all the magic powder I can."

"Ah-choo," baby Wendy
said again.

Grandma noticed the
magic powder all over the baby's
blanket. She began to brush
it off. Baby Wendy began to cry.

"Does that frighten you?"
Grandma asked. "I'll stop brushing
then."

Good, Wendy thought.
If enough powder sticks to my
blanket, I may be able to use it.

Several times baby Wendy
tried to switch back
into her own body. But
nothing happened, not even
a twinge.

But I have to keep trying,
Wendy thought.

She began to cry again.
Grandma hurried in to pick
her up. Magic powder flew
in every direction.

Then it was Sunday afternoon.
"When are Mom and Dad
coming home?" Miranda asked.

"In just a little while,"
Grandma said. "Before supper."

Before supper! baby
Wendy thought. There is not
much time left to switch.

She tried again and again.
Once she felt something.
But she did not have enough magic.

53

"Gurgle, glunk," baby Wendy
called to Grandma. Come and
shower me with some more powder,
she wanted to say.

"Will you rock the baby, dear?"
Grandma asked Miranda.
"I'm going to warm her bottle."

Miranda looked down at
baby Wendy.

Not you, Wendy thought.
I want Grandma and her magic powder.
Then she began to cry.

"There, there."
Grandma rushed in.
She picked up baby Wendy.
"I think she is spoiled,"
Miranda said.
"She's spoiled rotten."

"Listen, do I hear your folks?"
Grandma asked.
"Tell them to hurry. I do not
know what is the matter
with the baby."

Then baby Wendy began to cry
and yell and scream.

Miranda hurried out of
the room. Baby Wendy
continued to yell.
Grandma patted and burped her.
Magic powder flew.
It settled all over Wendy.
    Good, Wendy thought.
A little more powder, please.
    The front door opened.
Her mom and dad were coming.
    Oh, no, baby Wendy thought.
Now Grandma will go home.
I will never have enough
magic powder to switch back
into myself. I will try it
one more time.

"Magic power come my way.
Make me someone else today."
And then slowly Wendy felt
herself switch. She
slipped slowly back into
her own body just as her mom
picked up . . . baby Miranda!

"What's the matter, baby?"
her mom cooed into the baby's
soft neck. Baby Miranda
stopped crying.

Wendy sighed.
Wow, that was close, she thought.
She was back in her own body.
She was glad to be there.
It felt good, just like her own
monster pajamas would feel tonight.

Suddenly Wendy had an idea.
"Mom," she said. "Is it
all right if I pop some popcorn
the way you do it?
I think I have the magic now!"